THIS BOOK BELONGS TO

This edition published by HarperCollins Publishers Ltd 1999 for Silverdale Books
An imprint of Bookmart Ltd
Registered Number 2372865
Trading as Bookmart Limited
Desford Rd, Enderby, Leicester, LE9 5AD
First published 1958 by Sampson Lowe
© Darrell Waters Limited 1958 as to all text and illustrations
Enid Blyton's signature mark and the word 'NODDY' are Registered
Trade Marks of Enid Blyton Ltd
All rights reserved
ISBN 0 26 167250-9
Printed and bound in Italy

NODDY HAS
AN ADVENTURE

BY **Enid Blyton**

CONTENTS

"MILKO!" CALLED THE MILKMAN AT THE TOP
OF HIS VOICE

6

1. A VISIT FROM BIG-EARS

"OH what a long day I've had!" said little Noddy, finishing his supper. "I'm too tired to wash up the dirty dishes. I'll do them tomorrow morning."

He got up, yawning a very big yawn, and looked at his little bed.

> "I feel so sleepy
> And yawny and dozy
> And you, little bed,
> Look so lovely and cosy!
> I'll soon be cuddled
> Beneath your sheet,
> And fast asleep
> From my head to my feet!"

He cleaned his teeth and washed himself very well.

Then he sat down to take off his red shoes. He leaned back in his chair for a minute, and yawned again. And dear me, he fell fast asleep. His head nodded and his bell rang and jingled.

The jingling woke him up, and he opened his eyes and looked round. "What's that noise? Who's ringing a bell? Is it someone at the front door at this time of night?"

He got up and went to the door. No, there was no one there. "How silly I am—it was the bell on my hat ringing when I fell asleep and my head nodded!" said Noddy.

He put on his pyjamas, blew out his candle and jumped into his little bed. He snuggled down cosily.

> "It's dark and it's quiet,
> I'm going to sleep.
> My eyes are tight shut,
> They can't even peep.
> I'll dream of old Big-Ears,
> And dear Tessie Bear.

8

I'm going to Dreamland,
And now— —
I— —
am— —
THERE!"

And so he was, fast asleep, dreaming of having tea with Big-Ears and little Tessie Bear.

Noddy was very, very tired after his long and busy day, and he didn't even wake up the next morning when the milkman came and popped a bottle of milk down on the door-step.

"Milko!" called the milkman, wondering if little Noddy would come to the door and let him tap his head to make it nod, as he usually did. The milkman loved doing that. But this morning no Noddy appeared.

"Fast asleep, I suppose," said the milkman and went on his way, shouting "Milko" at the top

9

of his voice.

Someone else came to Noddy's house soon after that. Someone riding fast on a bicycle. It was Big-Ears, and he didn't look very pleased. He jumped off his bicycle, leant it against the wall of Noddy's house, and banged on the door.

"NODDY!" he called. "ARE YOU IN?"

Noddy woke with a start, and sat up in bed. "Oh Big-Ears! You made me jump!" he said. "What's the matter? Come in!"

Big-Ears opened the door and walked in. He looked so cross that Noddy stared at him in surprise.

"What's wrong, Big-Ears?" he said.

"Noddy, I want you to tell me something," said Big-Ears, sitting down in the chair. "Did

you play a trick on me last night?"

"Last night? No, of course not," said Noddy, in surprise. "I was so tired that I went to bed quite early, and I fell asleep at once—I've only just woken up. Whatever do you mean?"

10

"NODDY," SAID BIG-EARS, "I WANT YOU TO TELL
ME SOMETHING"

11

"Well—I woke up last night, and heard a car coming slowly up the woodland path to my front gate," said Big-Ears. "And it stopped there. I thought perhaps it was you, come to see me very late."

"Well, it wasn't," said Noddy. "And it wasn't *my* car either. That was fast asleep in its little garage. What happened? Did the car go away?"

"It stayed for a little while," said Big-Ears. "Then it suddenly said 'parp-parp' in exactly the same voice as yours does—and drove off!"

"Well, I don't see why you should come banging at my door and waking me up with a jump, just because someone stopped a car outside your house last night, Big-Ears," said Noddy. "You look so cross about it too!"

"Yes, but wait a bit," said Big-Ears. "When I went out into my garden this morning, I found that all the washing I'd left hanging out last night had been unpegged and taken away! Are you *sure* you didn't play a silly trick on me last night, Noddy?"

"NO," said Noddy, his head nodding up and down angrily, looking for all the world as if he were saying "YES". "I did NOT play a trick on you. And please go away, Big-Ears, if you're going to look as cross as that. I'm going to get dressed."

So Big-Ears got up, and went off without another word. Noddy ran to the window to watch him get on his bicycle and ride away.

"Well!" said Noddy. "He doesn't believe me! As if I'd do a silly thing like that! Now I'd better hurry up and get my car and go out, or I'll never make any money today."

2. NODDY HAS ANOTHER BUSY DAY

NODDY had a very busy day. First he took the clockwork mouse to the market to do his shopping.

"Clickity-click, I must be quick," said the little mouse. "Oh, you're sitting on my tail, Noddy."

"What a nuisance tails are!" said Noddy, pushing the mouse's tail away. "I'm glad *I* haven't got one. I'd cut it off if I had."

"Oooh, you wouldn't!" said the mouse, shocked.

"Have you heard my song about tails?" said Noddy, thinking of one at that very moment.

"No. And I don't want to hear it if it's rude," said the mouse. "Nor does my tail."

"It isn't rude. It's just funny, like your tail," said Noddy, and he began to sing.

14

"Oh tails are a nuisance,
And shouldn't be grown,
How thankful I am
That I've none of my own.
Tails, tails, tails!
Tails that wag,
Tails that drag,
Tails that wriggle and shake,
Tails that quiver,
Tails that shiver,
And tails that curl like a snake!
Oh tails are a nuisance,
And . . ."

"I think that's enough," said the clockwork mouse. "It's a silly song, not a funny one. Here's the market, Noddy. Let me get out. I've a good mind to charge you sixpence for making me listen to such a silly song."

Away he went, looking rather offended, his long thin tail wriggling behind him. Noddy laughed. "Oh dear — the clockwork mouse is very touchy.

15

Hallo, here's someone else who wants to hire my car. Good morning, Mrs Noah. How are all the animals?"

"They're all well and happy, except one of the elephants," said Mrs Noah, as they got into the car. "He's quarrelled with the lions, and he wants to leave the Ark. He keeps saying he will pack his trunk and go."

Noddy laughed and laughed, and almost knocked a lamp-post over. "I must remember to tell old Big-Ears about that," he said. And then he remembered that Big-Ears hadn't been very nice to him that morning. Oh dear— poor Big-Ears. Had he got his washing back yet?

Noddy took Mrs Noah back to the Ark, and then went to the station to meet the train. There was usually someone who wanted to hire his car when the train came in.

"Chuffity-chuffity-huffity-puffity!" The little toy train drew in at the platform, and plenty of

16

NODDY RAN TO COLLECT KATIE KITTEN'S LUGGAGE

17

passengers jumped out. One of them waved her umbrella at Noddy, and he ran to collect her luggage.

It was Katie Kitten, back from a visit to her Auntie Furry. She jumped into the car, and Noddy put her bag at the back. Off they went.

"Any news since I've been away?" asked Katie Kitten.

"Not much," said Noddy, "except that Martha Monkey climbed a tree to steal some apples, and tied her tail to a branch so that she wouldn't fall—and she couldn't untie the knot when she wanted to climb down again!"

"Oh—was she caught then?" said Katie, in delight. "She's always up to mischief."

"Yes. The farmer caught her," said Noddy. "Oh, and another piece of news is that someone took all Big-Ears' washing off the line last night—someone in a car. He thought I'd played a trick on him—but I wouldn't do a thing like that."

"No, of course not. I wonder who *did* take it, though," said Katie Kitten. "Here's my house,

18

Noddy. And here's sixpence for my fare. Goodbye!"

Out she got, and went into her little house with her bag. Noddy turned his car round and wondered if he should go and call on old Big-Ears. Perhaps he wouldn't be so cross now.

So off he went to Big-Ears' Toadstool House in the woods. He jumped out at the gate and went to the door and knocked. Then he saw a notice on the door.

GONE OUT. BACK TONIGHT.

"Oh bother!" said Noddy. "I *wonder* who came last night and took Big-Ears' washing. I'll look and see if there are any tyre marks outside the gate."

So he went to look, but he couldn't see any. The ground was much too hard and dry.

19

"Well—I'm going home," said Noddy, and got back into his car. "I've done a lot today and I'm tired and hungry. Oh dear—what a pity Big-Ears is out. I could have had tea with him and a nice rest. Wherever can he have gone? Perhaps he is looking for his washing!"

Away went Noddy to House-For-One, his bell jingling merrily. Now for a nice supper—then he would do his new jigsaw—and after that he would snuggle down into bed.

"And you can snuggle down in your garage, little car," said Noddy.

"Parp-parp," said the car, happily, and raced down the road at top speed. "Parp-parp!"

3. A VISIT FROM MR PLOD

NEXT morning, just as Noddy was busily washing his car, he saw Mr Plod the policeman coming along on his bicycle. Noddy waved his duster at him.

"Hallo, Mr Plod! Have you caught many robbers lately?"

"No. But I'm after one now," said Mr Plod, and jumped off his bicycle.

"Oooh, are you—how exciting!" said Noddy. "Who's the thief? What has he stolen?"

"He went to Mr Big-Bear's garden last night and picked all his lovely flowers," said Mr Plod. "Yes, every single one! I suppose he means

21

to sell them."

"Did Mr Big-Bear see the thief?" asked Noddy. "Why—he might have been the same fellow who stole Big-Ears' washing, Mr Plod!"

"He probably *was*," said Mr Plod. "He came in a car, Noddy, just as he did to Big-Ears' the night before!"

"Well, don't you dare say it was *my* car, Mr Plod!" said Noddy, fiercely. "Because it wasn't! I was in bed, and my car was in its garage."

"Mr Big-Bear said he heard it give a very quiet parp-parp in your car's voice," said Mr Plod. "Everyone knows the sound of your car's hooter, Noddy. Are you quite sure you're not playing tricks?"

Noddy was so cross that he actually stamped his foot at Mr Plod. The car was angry too and began to sound its hooter very loudly indeed. "PARP PARP PARP PARP PARP!"

"Now you be quiet," said Mr Plod to the car. "What with Noddy stamping around and you parping at me like that, I shall begin to lose my temper. Noddy, did you . . .?"

"I didn't, didn't, didn't!" said Noddy, not waiting for Mr Plod to finish his question.

"Noddy, will you please be quiet and let me ask you some qu . . ." began Mr Plod again.

"I won't, won't, won't!" cried Noddy.

Mr Plod took out his note-book and pencil. "Noddy, I must ask you if you were out last night," he said.

"I wasn't, wasn't, wasn't!" said Noddy and stamped his foot again.

"PARP PARP PARP!" said the car at the top of its voice.

"No more wasn'ts and won'ts and didn'ts, please," said Mr Plod sternly. "And no more parps from *you*, car, either."

And then someone suddenly ran joyfully up and jumped lovingly at Noddy, making Noddy sit down with a bump.

"Oh Bumpy-Dog — it's you!" he said. "Look — go and jump up at Mr Plod, not me!"

The Bumpy-Dog rushed at the surprised Mr Plod at once and leapt up at him, his tongue hanging out in excitement. Mr Plod sat down suddenly, too, and the Bumpy-Dog licked his face all over, and wouldn't let him get up.

"DON'T!" roared Mr Plod at Bumpy. But Bumpy never seemed to know what "Don't" meant, and every time the policeman tried to get up, Bumpy leapt at him and made him sit down with a bump again.

"I'll lock you up, you pest of a dog!" shouted Mr Plod. "Noddy, call him off!"

"Bumpy — come here," said Noddy, and Bumpy left Mr Plod and ran at once to Noddy, who fell over again as Bumpy sprang at him lovingly. Noddy put his arms round Bumpy's neck and whispered to him. "Chase Mr Plod away, Bumpy, please!"

24

THE BUMPY-DOG RUSHED AT MR PLOD AND LEAPT
UP AT HIM

25

So, as soon as Mr Plod got up, Bumpy chased him excitedly, barking all the time. Mr Plod disappeared very quickly indeed round the next corner. Noddy heaved a sigh of relief.

"I don't like this business of someone going round robbing people at night in a car that sounds like mine," he thought.

"Oh hallo—here's dear little Tessie Bear—and Bumpy again. Down, Bumpy, down! Oh my goodness, what a dog!"

"Hallo, little Noddy," said Tessie Bear. "Bumpy and I have come to see you. What's the matter with Mr Plod? He came round the corner at sixty miles an hour and nearly knocked me over."

"Come indoors and I'll tell you, Tessie," said Noddy, giving her a hug. "We'll have some lemonade and a bun. No, *not* you, Bumpy. Keep off, I tell you! Good gracious, I seem to be sitting down all the time when you're around!"

4. TESSIE HAS A PLAN

NODDY and Tessie Bear were soon enjoying lemonade and buns. Bumpy sat in a third chair, wagging his tail all the time. Thumpity-thumpity-thump it went against the back of the chair.

Noddy told Tessie Bear about Big-Ears and his stolen washing, and about Mr Big-Bear's flowers.

"All picked and taken away!" said Noddy. "And Mr Big-Bear heard a car saying 'parp-parp' like mine does, but very, very quietly. And they *both* think it might be me playing tricks! Playing tricks! Good gracious, that isn't playing tricks, it's stealing."

"Oh dear," said Tessie Bear, nibbling her bun.

"You'll have to do something about it, Noddy, before people begin to think it must be you. Everybody knows the parp-parp noise your car makes. It isn't a bit like anyone else's car. Do you suppose someone is borrowing your hooter?"

"Good gracious, no!" said Noddy. "I would miss it if they did. It's always on my car each morning. Besides my garage is locked when the car is there. Bumpy, stop licking the sugar off those buns!"

"Wuff, wuff," said Bumpy, and jumped down from his chair. He tried to get on Noddy's knee.

"Oh do get down," said Noddy. "Tessie, did you ever know such a licky dog? I shall have to get a towel and wipe off his licks. My hanky is too small. Down, Bumpy, down!"

28

"Bumpy!" said Tessie in a stern voice that Noddy had never heard before. To Noddy's surprise Bumpy stopped prancing about, lay down, put his head on his paws, and stayed quite still.

"However do you make him do that, Tessie?" said Noddy astonished. "What a wonderful thing! You really are clever. Have another bun. Or would you like a biscuit?"

At the word "biscuit" Bumpy shot to his feet again, and leapt on Noddy with a glad wuff.

"Oh *don't!*" said Noddy. "Just as I was praising you, too. For goodness' sake go out into the garden, Bumpy."

He shooed Bumpy into the garden and shut the door. Bumpy immediately put his head in at the window, with his two front paws resting on the window-sill.

"All right. Stay there and listen to everything," said Noddy. "But DON'T come in."

"Noddy," said Tessie Bear, "do you suppose someone is borrowing your car at night — getting into your garage, and driving it out — then putting it back again?"

"Oh no, Tessie," said Noddy. "I told you my

29

garage is *locked* each night. And, anyway, if anyone tried to take my car it would hoot and hoot,
and wake me up."

"Yes, of course," said Tessie. "Well, look,
Noddy, you come and stay with me tonight, and
then if anything is stolen, and anyone hears a
parp-parp noise, we can PROVE it wasn't
you."

"Oh Tessie—that *is* a good idea," said Noddy,
pleased. "But wait! I don't really like leaving
my little house empty—because if there *is* a
robber about, he might come and steal *my*
things!"

"Well, why not leave Bumpy here to guard everything," said Tessie. She turned to Bumpy, who
was listening at the window. "You'd like

to guard Noddy's
house, wouldn't you,
Bumpy-Dog?"

Bumpy was so over-
joyed at being spoken
to again that he leapt
in at the window and
rushed to lick Tessie.
"Wuff!" he said happily.
"Wuff-wuff-WUFF!" Then

30

NODDY FLAPPED BUMPY AWAY WITH A CUSHION

he tried to lick Noddy, but Noddy was ready for him and flapped him away with a cushion.

"In that case, Tessie," said Noddy, "I *will* come and spend the night at your house, and we'll leave Bumpy here. I'll leave my car here too, because you haven't got a garage. Now I'd better get the car out and go and do some work. Would you like to come with me?"

"I'll come as far as the shops, then I must go home and make up a bed for you, Noddy," said Tessie. "It *will* be nice having you to stay. Let Bumpy come with you in your car, and then you can bring him back here when you put your car away for the night."

So away went Noddy, Tessie and Bumpy in the

car. Bumpy sat at the back, poking his head between them, enjoying himself.

Noddy dropped Tessie off at the shops, and then began to

look out for passengers as usual. First of all he took Miss Fluffy Cat, then he took Mr Noah, then Mr Toy Dog and then Sally Skittle. But all of them said that Bumpy was a dreadful nuisance, sitting at the back.

"Licking my head all over!" complained Sally Skittle. "Why doesn't he take a job at the post-office and lick stamps all the time? *Must* you have him with you, Noddy?"

"Just for today," said Noddy, and helped Sally Skittle out of his car. Bumpy at once slid down into the seat beside Noddy. He felt very, very grand sitting there!

"I really don't know why I like such a tiresome dog," said Noddy. "No, *don't* wag your tail like that—there isn't room on the front seat. Sit on it, Bumpy, sit on it."

5. QUITE A LOT HAPPENS

THAT evening, after Noddy had finished his day's work, he drove home, and put his car into the garage. He locked the door, and went to wash and make himself tidy before going to Tessie's house.

The Bumpy-Dog watched him, with his tail down. He knew the time had come when he had to stay in Noddy's house alone and guard it. "Wuff," he said, in a small, sad voice.

"I'll leave you some dog food to eat," said Noddy, putting a dish down. "Oh BUMPY! Don't gobble so. Good gracious, dog, you've swallowed the whole lot already! You can't even have tasted it! What a shame! Well, you won't have anything else — except this bone."

Bumpy sprang at the bone in delight, and lay

down peacefully gnawing it, while Noddy got himself ready. Then Noddy patted Bumpy and hurried out of the door before he could rush out with him. "Wuff," said Bumpy again, very sadly.

Noddy went off to Tessie Bear's and had a very pleasant evening indeed. Tessie had made a lovely supper, and afterwards they played snap with Tessie's uncle and aunt.

Tessie's Uncle Bear won easily. Then he told Noddy about three relations of his, called The Three Bears, whose home had been visited by a naughty little girl.

"And she sat down in their chairs and broke one, and she tasted their porridge and ate some all up, and then she went to sleep on one of their beds," said Uncle Bear.

Noddy was shocked. What a badly behaved little girl! Tessie yawned. She had heard her uncle tell the story of The Three Bears a great many times.

"Go to bed, now," said Uncle Bear. "You're tired, both of you. Tessie, show Noddy his little bedroom."

It was fun to sleep in someone else's house. Noddy liked it. He was soon fast asleep. Tessie Bear woke him in the morning.

"Get up, Noddy!" she said. "There's been *another* robbery in the night— someone has picked all Mr Sparks' ripe plums. But NOBODY can say it was you playing a trick, because you were here. Did you hear it raining in the night?"

"No. I didn't hear anything at all," said Noddy, still sleepy. "Good gracious—fancy Mr Sparks' plums being stolen! Well, I'm glad I slept here, and not at home! Mr Plod is sure to hurry round to my house and say the robber had a car that went parp-parp like mine!"

Noddy went to fetch his car after breakfast,

wondering how the Bumpy-Dog had got on in the night.

He had quite a shock when he arrived at House-For-One. Big-Ears was there—and Mr Plod—and Mr Tubby Bear—and Mr Sparks!

"Whatever are you all here for?" asked Noddy.

"My plums were stolen in the night!" said Mr Sparks, fiercely. "And I heard a car drive up—and when it stopped it said 'parp-parp' just like yours!"

"Well, I stayed the night at Tessie Bear's house," said Noddy. "So there! Her aunt and uncle will tell you. And what is more, I didn't even have my car with me. I left it locked in my garage. So it WASN'T me, and it WASN'T my car!"

"Dear me—is that so?" said Mr Plod, surprised. "Well, I must say I'm glad to hear that. Of course if you were staying at Tessie Bear's house, you couldn't have taken Mr Sparks' plums."

"Anyway, it's not like our Noddy to *steal* things," said Big-Ears. "I thought he might have taken my washing for a bit of fun—but he certainly wouldn't steal Mr Big-Bear's flowers or Mr Sparks' plums."

"Wuff-wuff-wuff!" barked the Bumpy-Dog from inside Noddy's house. He flung himself against the door and it shook from top to bottom.

"Don't, Bumpy, don't! You'll break it down!" cried Noddy, and ran to unlock the door. Bumpy came out like a bullet from a gun and flung himself rapturously on everyone. They all went down like skittles, even Big-Ears. Then Bumpy ran round licking everyone with joy, his tail thumping against them as he went.

"GO HOME TO TESSIE BEAR, YOU RUDE, ROUGH DOG!" commanded Mr Plod, in such a fierce voice that even Big-Ears quaked in his shoes. Bumpy put his tail down and shot off at once. Everyone heaved sighs of relief.

"Well, I'll be going," said Mr Plod. "Sorry to have been cross with you yesterday, Noddy. I only hope I catch the thief before he does any more damage. Coming, Mr Sparks and Mr Tubby Bear? We may as well go along together. What about you Big-Ears?"

"I'll stay and have a talk with Noddy," said Big-Ears. "This is all very, very peculiar!"

Big-Ears was very nice to Noddy. He was sorry for saying that Noddy had taken his washing.

Noddy went to open his garage to take out his car.

"I'll run you back to your house, Big-Ears," he said. "As you haven't got your bicycle with you."

He swung open the garage doors—and then stared in amazement. "Big-Ears—look! What's happened to my car? It's covered with mud! It's DREADFULLY dirty! Oh, Big-Ears, what *can* have happened? It was quite clean when I left it here last night!"

6. NODDY HAS A WONDERFUL IDEA

BIG-EARS was most astonished to see such a dirty little car. It gave a tiny hoot as they looked at it. "Parp-parp."

"Why don't you hoot properly?" said Noddy, surprised, and went to look at the hooter. "Oh, Big-Ears, LOOK! Someone has tied string very tightly round and round the rubber hooter, so that it can't hoot properly!"

"Noddy! The thief comes here each night and takes *your* car!" cried Big-Ears. "He must have a key to your garage. He ties up the hooter each night so that it can't hoot loudly and give him away—but it just manages to hoot a very small 'parp-parp' and that's what's made everyone think it was *your* car— with you driving it!"

"And it's all muddy because the thief took it out in the rain last night!" said Noddy. "And LOOK—here's a plum. That *shows* that someone took my car up to Mr Sparks' orchard last night. Big-Ears—who can it be?"

Mrs Tubby Bear came to speak to them. "What's the matter?" she said. "I heard the Bumpy-Dog barking at the top of his voice in the middle of the night. He woke us all up."

"Oh dear—what a pity you didn't go and find out why he was barking," said Big-Ears.

"Well, I thought Noddy was at home," said Mrs Tubby Bear. "Do tell me what has happened."

So they told her, and she was most surprised. "Your poor car!" she said to Noddy. "It must have hated being taken away by someone else each night. How did the thief get a key to your garage, Noddy?"

"Well, I had two keys, and I lost one a week ago," said Noddy. "So I expect the thief found it. Big-Ears—how can we catch him? Do you think he'll come again tonight?"

"Yes, I expect so," said Big-Ears. "We shall have to watch for him. But it's no good watching inside your house, Noddy. We'd never be outside quickly enough to get him. We must watch from somewhere outside."

"But where?" said Noddy, looking up and down the road. "There's nowhere we can hide and still watch my garage at the same time."

"No, there isn't," said Big-Ears, frowning. "It's a pity there isn't a post-box anywhere near. We could have hidden behind that."

"We could make one, Big-Ears!" said Noddy, his head nodding up and down excitedly. "I don't mean a big heavy one. But can't we get some big sheets of paper, and paint them red, and roll them up to look like post-boxes— *two*—one for me and one for you?"

"Yes—what a good idea! Yes, of course we could!" said Big-Ears. "And we'll paint your dustbin lid red to make a top to one post-box, and perhaps Mrs Tubby Bear would lend us her dustbin lid too, for the second post-box."

"And we'll make slits, like all post-boxes have for posting letters in!" cried Noddy, dancing about in joy. "And we'll peep through those and keep watch. Oh, Big-Ears, what a WONDERFUL idea. Let's get some stiff paper and red paint and start straight away!"

Well, before the morning was over, two very life-like post-boxes stood in Noddy's back garden! They were made of stiff paper, painted scarlet, with

NODDY AND BIG-EARS STARTED STRAIGHT AWAY TO
MAKE TWO POST-BOXES

red dustbin lids on top—and each had a nice wide slit, which looked as if it were meant for letters—but which was really for Noddy and Big-Ears to peep through!

"Shall we borrow Bumpy-Dog and let him sleep in the car tonight?" said Noddy, his head nodding again. "That will stop the thief taking the car and driving away before we can stop him. I don't want to lose my car, you know!"

"You are full of good ideas, Noddy," said Big-Ears, pleased. "Yes, we'll fetch him tonight. I'll get him if you like. This is going to be *fun*, Noddy!"

7. WHEN THE MOON SHONE OUT

NODDY cleaned up his car in the afternoon and then went out to see if he could find any passengers. Big-Ears went shopping and bought a jam sponge and some little cakes for tea, and a big box of chocolates. He wanted to make a fuss of Noddy because he hadn't been very kind to him a day or two before.

They had a lovely tea together, and then Big-Ears played cards with Noddy until it got dark. "As soon as it is *really* dark we will take out our pretend post-boxes," said Big-Ears. "The moon will be up later on, and we shall easily be able to keep a watch on your garage. I think I'd better slip up to Tessie Bear's now and fetch Bumpy."

So Big-Ears fetched Bumpy who was most surprised and pleased to see Noddy again. He rushed at him in joy, but Noddy skipped behind a chair.

"No, Bumpy! I am *not* going to be bumped over any more today. Lie down! Be quiet! Keep still! Good gracious, don't you understand *any* of those orders? Sit still and I'll sing you a song about yourself. I said SIT STILL!"

So Bumpy sat still, pricked up his ears and listened while Noddy sang to him.

"He barks and he jumps,
His tail wags and thumps,
He leaps in the air like a frog!
He barks and he runs,
He gobbles up buns,
This bumpity, thumpity, jumpity,
terrible DOG!"

Big-Ears laughed, and Bumpy gave a delighted bark and flung himself on Noddy. But Noddy was still behind the chair. "No!" he said. "If you knock me over I'll *never* sing your song again. Never. Behave yourself!"

Soon Big-Ears saw that it was really dark. "Time to take out our post-boxes, Noddy," he said, so out they went with them, secretly and quietly. Noddy put his down across the road, and Big-Ears put his not far from Noddy's house. They each got inside their own, putting them over their heads and sliding them down carefully over their bodies. Ah—now they could easily peer through the slits at the top, just under the red-painted dustbin lids.

Noddy's head was nodding so fast with excitement that the bell on his hat kept ringing, and he had to stop nodding. It would never do to give a warning to the thief!

The moon came up, and soon it was quite light. Noddy and Big-Ears could easily see Noddy's garage. Inside, curled up in the car, was the Bumpy-

Dog, very quiet and still. He had been told exactly what to do.

Nothing happened for a long, long time. Then Noddy heard footsteps, and his head began to nod again. His bell rang, and he heard a loud "SHHHHHSH!" from the post-box across the road. Even Big-Ears could hear his bell!

The footsteps came nearer and passed by Big-Ears' post-box. He peered out of the slit. Ah— it was only old Jumbo taking an evening stroll.

Then they heard more footsteps—who was it this time? Noddy peered out of his slit—goodness, it was Mr Plod! There he was, pacing slowly by. And just as he passed by Noddy's box, Noddy sneezed.

"A-whoooshhhoo!"

Mr Plod was very startled indeed. He looked all round but he couldn't see anyone at all. Who had sneezed? It had sounded so very close. He looked at the red post-box. No—post-boxes don't sneeze. Still—how very extraordinary!

MR PLOD WAS VERY STARTLED. HE LOOKED ALL ROUND
BUT HE COULDN'T SEE ANYONE AT ALL

Mr Plod went on his way, much to Noddy's relief. Noddy had been rather afraid Mr Plod would lean against his post-box—then it would certainly have tipped over!

Time went on. The moon climbed a little higher and then went behind a thick cloud. Now was the time for a thief to come—while it was so dark.

Big-Ears thought he heard something. Yes— someone passed by his post-box like a shadow! Then Noddy's sharp ears heard the sound of a little click—someone was unlocking his garage door! There wasn't a sound from the Bumpy-Dog—he had been told not to bark until he saw the thief.

Then everything happened at once. Oh, WHAT excitement! Noddy's head began to nod again, and his bell jingled out loudly. Big-Ears shouted, and Bumpy barked. "Stop thief, stop thief!" Wuff-wuff-WUFF! Jingle, jingle! "Hey, there, stop! WHO ARE YOU?"

8. WHAT A CHASE!

THE thief had crept into the garage. He had got into the driving-seat. And then the Bumpy-Dog had leapt at him, and barked at the top of his voice!

In a terrible fright the thief sprang out of the car and rushed to the garage door. He managed to shut it on Bumpy's nose and then tore off down the street.

"After him!" yelled Big-Ears. The thief turned round at the shout and in great alarm saw two red post-boxes bobbing down the road after him.

Two post-boxes—with feet underneath! He was so frightened that he didn't even look where he was going. He fled round the corner, and

bumped full tilt into Mr Plod, who was just coming back. CRASH! They both fell over backwards. Mr Plod sat up angrily.

"Now then—what . . . good gracious! Am I going mad—or can I see two post-boxes running about? I'm dreaming! And who's this fellow who knocked me over? Hey, you, come back!"

Mr Plod ran after the thief, and the post-boxes ran after them both. Mr Plod was dreadfully scared of them, and the thief was just as scared of Mr Plod. Mr Tubby Bear, coming back from a party, couldn't think *what* was happening. He scurried home at top speed when the two post-boxes went by. No wonder letters often got lost in the post, if *that* was the kind of thing post-boxes did at night!

The thief was getting away. Mr Plod was too fat to run fast, and Noddy and Big-Ears found the post-boxes were difficult to run in. "Oh dear!" panted Noddy. "We can't catch him!"

But just then something shot past him like a rocket, barking excitedly. It was the Bumpy-

54

MR PLOD RAN AFTER THE THIEF, AND THE POST-BOXES
RAN AFTER THEM BOTH

Dog! He had managed to squeeze his nose into the crack of the garage door, and swing it open.

WUFF-WUFF-WUFF! What a chase!

Well, Bumpy caught the thief just as he had got to the river. There was a little boat there, all ready for the robber to sail away in. It was still half full of the plums he had piled there last night!

Bumpy leapt at him and down he went. Then Bumpy sat firmly on top of him, his tail going thump-thump-thump with joy. Up came Mr Plod, panting. And some way behind came the red post-boxes, their feet running fast beneath them.

"Keep that fellow safe for me, Bumpy-Dog," ordered Mr Plod, "while I find out what these post-boxes are doing. What peculiar goings-on! Now then, you two post-boxes, what's the meaning of this?"

Big-Ears wriggled out of his post-box, and then Noddy slid out of his. Mr Plod stared in amazement. "What! Noddy and Big-Ears! What do you think you're doing?"

"The same as you—chasing the thief!" said Big-Ears, cheerfully. "Who is he? My word— it's Sammy Sailor-Doll! Well, who would have thought it! Shame on you, Sammy—taking Noddy's car and going out robbing people at night! Get off him, Bumpy-Dog. Mr Plod's going to lock him up."

"Oh no, oh no!" said Sammy Sailor-Doll, and he knelt down in front of Mr Plod.

"Oh yes, oh yes," said Mr Plod. "Get up at once! Pretending you're sorry like that! Big-Ears, let's put him inside one of your peculiar post-boxes—he can't possibly try to run away if he's in one of those. It will be an easy way of taking him to the police-station!"

So off they went with the sailor doll inside a red post-box, the dustbin lid still on top. He

didn't like it at all—and he didn't like the Bumpy-Dog sniffing around his ankles either!

On the way they passed Tessie Bear's house. "Oh — let's take Bumpy back to her—and tell her all that's happened," said Noddy. "Look—they're still up, there's a light on!"

"All right—we'll do that," said Big-Ears, who was longing to tell someone all their exciting news. "We'll take the other post-box with us and show Tessie's aunt and uncle how we hid inside it. Come on Bumpy—and do stop thumping your tail round my legs. I know you're pleased with yourself—but you very nearly didn't get out of Noddy's garage, you know!"

And soon Noddy, Big-Ears and the Bumpy-Dog were all in Tessie Bear's house, drinking hot cocoa and eating chocolate biscuits, and telling their exciting tale.

"Oh I *wish* I'd been there!" said little Tessie Bear, looking perfectly sweet in her dressing-gown. "I'm *glad* the thief has been caught. How I'd like to have seen you rushing along in the post-boxes!"

"WUFF WUFF!" said the Bumpy-Dog, putting a big paw on Noddy's knee.

"No, you can't have any more chocolate biscuits," said Tessie. "You've had five already, and you can't have a bun either."

"He doesn't want a bun or a biscuit!" said Noddy. "He wants me to sing you his Special Song. Listen, Tessie! This is the song of the Bumpy-Dog.

59

"He barks and he jumps,
His tail wags and thumps,
He leaps in the air like a frog!
He barks and he runs,
He gobbles up buns,
This bumpity, thumpity, jumpity,
terrible DOG!

Now altogether:

This bumpity, thumpity, jumpity,
terrible DOG!"

Everyone yelled the last line at the tops of their voices, and the Bumpy-Dog leapt at Noddy in delight. You can guess what Noddy said, I expect.

"Oh, DON'T, Bumpy-Dog! DON'T!"